little grasshopper books™

Bedtime Stories

Get the App!

1. Download the Little Grasshopper Library App* from the App Store or Google Play. Find direct links to store locations at **www.littlegrasshopperbooks.com**

2. Open the app and tap the **+ Add Book** button at the bottom of the screen.**

3. Line up the QR Code Scanner with one of the QR codes found in this book. Each story will automatically start downloading to your app!

4. Be sure to accept any prompts that come up.

5. Information on device compatibility and troubleshooting can be found at **www.littlegrasshopperbooks.com**

Based on the classic tale; illustrated by: Stacy Peterson, Amanda Gulliver, Dan Crisp, Emma Trithart, Jean Claude, Morgan Huff, and Tracy Cottingham.
App content developed in partnership with Filament Games.

Louis Weber, CEO
West Side Publishing, Inc.
8140 Lehigh Avenue
Morton Grove, IL 60053

ISBN: 978-1-64030-983-8
Manufactured in China.
8 7 6 5 4 3 2 1

*We reserve the right to terminate the apps.
**Smartphone not included. Standard data rates may apply to download. Once the app and an individual book's content are downloaded, the app does not use data or require Wi-Fi access.

Table of Contents

little grasshopper books™

Country Mouse, City Mouse

4

A city mouse took a trip on a train to see the country.
He looked out the window and thought that the view was
very pretty, even if it was not quite as fancy as his city.

In the country, he made a new friend, a kind
and lovely country mouse. The country mouse
asked him to dinner. He was happy to go to her
warm, bright house and meet her friends.

Everyone brought simple, tasty food to share. The city mouse was used to more fancy food. He ate some to be polite, but it was not his favorite.

Everyone talked and played games. One by one,
the country mouse's friends left, saying how delightful it
had been to meet the city mouse.

As the city mouse left, he said, "Someday, you must come to the city to have dinner at my house with my friends!" She said she would love to visit soon.

At the train station, the country
mouse gave the city mouse a bundle
of bread and cheese for his trip.

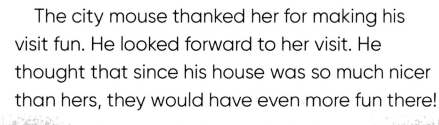

The city mouse thanked her for making his visit fun. He looked forward to her visit. He thought that since his house was so much nicer than hers, they would have even more fun there!

For one whole month, the country mouse saved up money for her special trip. Then she rode the train to the city. She brought pretty wildflowers from her yard and cheese from a local farm. She arrived in the city and found her way through busy streets.

At his house, the city mouse welcomed his friend and thanked her for her gifts. But he set them on a table and forgot about them. He did not put the flowers in a vase or look at the cheese.

Instead, he showed her his home so
she could admire it. He had a huge,
fancy table of expensive cheese.

His friends said hello, but they went back to talking to each other and the city mouse. The country mouse felt so sad. She liked the nice cheese, but it was not fun to eat all alone.

Her friend's house was pretty, but it was not very cozy. After a short time, the country mouse tried to sneak out of the party.

The country mouse reached for the
door handle. Then she heard the city
mouse. "Where are you going?" he
asked. "The party isn't over!"

"Thank you for inviting me, but I'm not having very much fun," she said. "No one is talking to me, and I miss my friends at home."

"I'm sorry!" the city mouse said. "I was trying to impress you, but I didn't act like a very good friend." He asked her to stay so they could play her favorite game.

The other mice wanted to play too! They all talked, laughed, and had fun together. The city mouse passed around a plate of the country mouse's special cheese.

At the end of the party, the country mouse thanked the city mouse. She was happy to return to her cozy home and simple life. But she was happy that she had a city friend now, too.

Whole Duty of Children

A child should always say what's true
And speak when he is spoken to,
And behave mannerly at table,
At least as far as he is able.

Infant Joy

I have no name
I am but two days old.—
What shall I call thee?
I happy am
Joy is my name,—
Sweet joy befall thee!

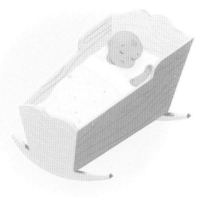

Pretty joy!
Sweet joy but two days old,
Sweet joy I call thee;
Thou dost smile.
I sing the while
Sweet joy befall thee.

Rock-a-Bye, Baby

Rock-a-bye, baby,
On the tree tops,
When the wind blow,
The cradle will rock.

When the bough breaks,
The cradle will fall,
Down will come baby
Cradle and all.

The Fog

The fog comes
on little cat feet.

It sits looking
over harbor and city
on silent haunches
and then moves on.

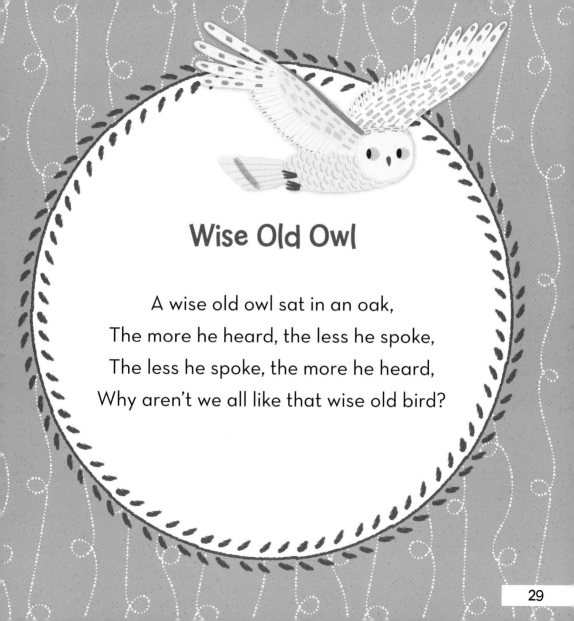

Wise Old Owl

A wise old owl sat in an oak,
The more he heard, the less he spoke,
The less he spoke, the more he heard,
Why aren't we all like that wise old bird?

Little Red Riding Hood

Once upon a time there was a little girl whom everyone called Little Red Riding Hood because she always wore her red hooded cloak.

One morning her mother asked Little Red Riding
Hood to take a basket of cookies to her grandmother.

"Go straight to Grandma's house and do not talk to any strangers," her mother warned.

"Yes, Mom," Little Red Riding Hood promised.

Little Red Riding Hood did not do as her mother asked. She stopped along the way to pick flowers. A wolf suddenly appeared.

"What are you doing, little girl?" Wolf asked.

"I am going to visit my grandmother," Little Red Riding Hood answered.

"Where does your grandmother live?" asked Wolf.

"She lives in the little house on the other side of the forest," Little Red Riding Hood replied.

"Have a nice visit," Wolf said and waved goodbye.
Little Red Riding Hood picked more flowers.

Wolf ran as fast as he could to Grandma's house. He knocked lightly on the door.

"Who is there?" Grandma asked.

"Little Red Riding Hood," Wolf replied in a sweet voice.

"Come in, my dear," Grandma said.
Wolf pounced on Grandma and ate her in a single bite.

Wolf put on Grandma's spare nightgown and climbed into bed.

Little Red Riding Hood knocked on Grandma's door a short time later.

"Are you there, Grandma?" she called out. "I brought you cookies."

When she heard no answer, Little Red Riding Hood opened the door and walked in.

Something was wrong.

"Grandma, what big
ears you have," said
Little Red Riding Hood.
"All the better to hear
you with," said Wolf.

"Grandma, what big
eyes you have," said
Little Red Riding Hood.
"All the better to see
you with," said Wolf.

"Grandma, what a big nose you have," said Little Red Riding Hood.

"All the better to smell you with," said Wolf.

"But Grandma! What big teeth you have!" she said.
"All the better to eat you with!" Wolf growled.

"Help!" Little Red Riding Hood yelled.

Little Red Riding Hood's father was outside and heard her scream. He rushed into the house.

He saw Wolf's big belly and guessed what
happened. Her father jumped on Wolf and out flew
Grandma. Luckily, Grandma was not hurt.

Her father chased Wolf far away.
Little Red Riding Hood never spoke to a stranger again.

At the Zoo

First I saw the white bear, then I saw the black,
Then I saw the camel with a hump upon his back,
Then I saw the grey wolf, with mutton in his maw,
Then I saw the wombat waddle in the straw,
Then I saw the elephant a-waving of his trunk,
Then I saw the monkeys—
Mercy, how unpleasantly they smelt!

Mary's Lamb

Mary had a little lamb,
Its fleece was white as snow,
And everywhere that Mary went
The lamb was sure to go,
He followed her to school one day—
That was against the rule,
It made the children laugh and play,
To see a lamb at school.

And so the Teacher turned him out,
But still he lingered near,
And waited patiently about,
Till Mary did appear,
And then he ran to her, and laid
His head upon her arm,
As if he said—"I'm not afraid—
You'll keep me from all harm."

"What makes the lamb love Mary so?"
The eager children cry—

"O, Mary loves the lamb, you know,"
The Teacher did reply,—
"And you each gentle animal
In confidence may bind,
And make them follow at your call,
If you are always kind."

This Little Piggy

This little piggy went to market,

This little piggy stayed home,

This little piggy had roast beef,

This little piggy had none.

This little piggy went...
Wee, wee, wee, all the way home!

little grasshopper books™

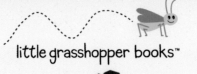

The Three Little Pigs

There was once a mother pig who sent her three little pigs out into the world to start their lives.

The first little pig bought some straw and built a home.

A wolf came along and said, "Little Pig, Little Pig, let me come in."

The first little pig replied, "Not by the hair on my chinny chin chin!"

"Then I'll huff, and I'll puff, and I'll blow your house down!" the wolf said. He huffed, and he puffed, and he blew down the straw house. The first little pig ran away.

The second little pig bought some sticks and built a home.

The wolf came along and said, "Little Pig, Little Pig, let me come in."

The second little pig replied, "Not by the hair on my chinny chin chin!"

"Then I'll huff, and I'll puff, and I'll blow your house down!" the wolf said. He huffed, and he puffed, and he blew down the stick house. The second little pig ran away.

The third little pig bought some bricks and built a home. The wolf came along and said, "Little Pig, Little Pig, let me come in!"

The third little pig replied, "Not by the hair on my chinny chin chin!"

"Then I'll huff, and I'll puff, and I'll blow your house down!" the wolf said. The wolf huffed, and he puffed, but he could not blow down the brick house.

The wolf thought he might be able to trick the pig into leaving his house. "Let's pick apples tomorrow," he said.

The pig said, "Okay." He woke up early and went to the orchard alone.

When the wolf got to the orchard, he asked, "Little Pig, why did you not wait for me?" The pig said nothing. "Will you at least throw me an apple?" asked the wolf. The pig threw an apple as far as he could to get rid of the wolf.

"Little pig, would you like to go to the fair tomorrow?" the wolf asked. The pig said, "Okay." He woke up early and went to the fair alone. At the fair, he bought a new bucket. As the pig was walking home, he spotted the wolf. With nowhere to hide, the pig got inside his bucket.

The bucket rolled down the hill toward the wolf. The wolf ran screaming to the pig's home.

"Little Pig! Something scary just chased me down the hill!"

The pig laughed, "It was me in a bucket."

The wolf thought he might be able to get into the pig's home through the chimney. The pig was not worried. He filled his bucket with ice water and placed it in the fireplace.

The wolf came down the chimney and fell right into the cold water. The wolf was so embarrassed that he ran away and never came back.

The third little pig heard a knock on his door. It was the other two little pigs! The three little pigs lived happily ever after in the brick house.

Who Has Seen the Wind?

Who has seen the wind?
Neither I nor you.
But when the leaves hang trembling,
The wind is passing through.
Who has seen the wind?
Neither you nor I.
But when the trees bow down their heads,
The wind is passing by.

The Rainbow

Boats sail on the rivers,
And ships sail on the seas;
But clouds that sail across the sky
Are prettier than these.

There are bridges on the rivers,
As pretty as you please;
But the bow that bridges heaven,
And overtops the trees,
And builds a road from earth to sky,
Is prettier far than these.

Itsy, Bitsy Spider

The itsy, bitsy spider
Went up the water spout.

Down came the rain
And washed the spider out.

Out came the sun
And dried up all the rain.

Now the itsy, bitsy spider
Climbs up the spout again.

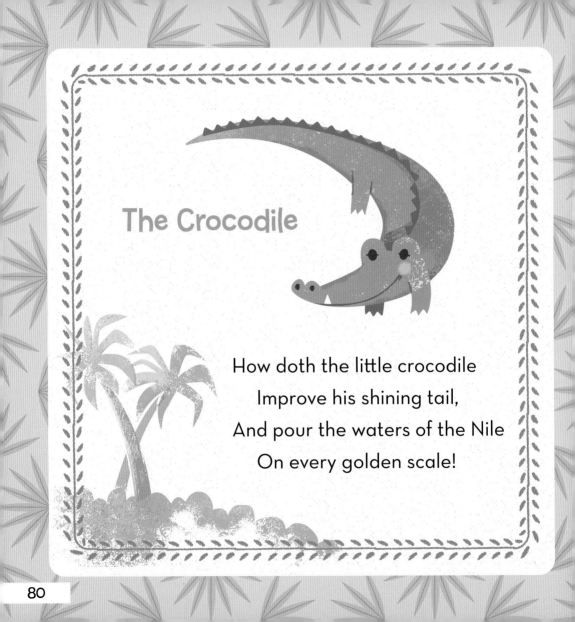

The Crocodile

How doth the little crocodile
Improve his shining tail,
And pour the waters of the Nile
On every golden scale!

How cheerfully he seems to grin,
How neatly spreads his claws,
And welcomes little fishes in,
With gently smiling jaws.

little grasshopper books™

The Little Red Hen

A Little Red Hen lived in a barnyard with her chicks.
They all loved to eat big, fat, juicy worms.

The Little Red Hen walked around the barnyard gathering yummy worms. She walked past the Cat, taking a nap. She walked past the Rat, nibbling corn.

She walked right past the Pig in his sty. He was always eating when she walked by.

One day the Little Red Hen found something she had not seen before. She did not know what it was! The Cat did not know either. He went back to sleep with a great big snore. The Rat did not know. He went back to his hole.

The Pig said, "It's a seed. If you plant it, it grows into wheat. Wheat can make flour. Flour can make bread."

"We should plant the seed!" said the Little Red Hen. But she was always so busy. She did not have time to plant it. She asked, "Who will plant the seed?"

The Cat said, "Not I."

The Rat said, "Not I."

The Pig said, "Not I."

"Well, then," said the Little Red Hen, "I will."
And she did.

All summer, the Little Red Hen watched the wheat grow tall. One day, she asked, "Who will cut the wheat?"

The Cat said, "Not I."

The Rat said, "Not I."

The Pig said, "Not I."

"Well, then," said the Little Red Hen, "I will."
And she did.

Then the Little Red Hen called out,
"Who will thresh this wheat?"

"Not I", they said.

So the Little Red Hen sighed and said,
"Well, I guess I will."

The Little Red Hen threshed the grain. Then she called out, "Who will carry the wheat to the mill to be ground?"

The Cat said, "Not I."
The Rat said, "Not I."
The Pig said, "Not I."

So the Little Red Hen could do nothing but say, "I will."
And she did.

The Little Red Hen walked all the way to the mill. Then she walked all the way home with a big sack of flour. She asked, "Who will make the bread?"

The Cat said, "Not I."
The Rat said, "Not I."
The Pig said, "Not I."

So the Little Red Hen said once more, "I will," and she did.

The Little Red Hen put on her apron and her cap. She got the dough ready. She put the bread in the oven. She watched it bake.

The smell was
so good it woke the
Cat from his nap.

The Pig said, "Mmm, food."

The Rat sat up and ran
toward the kitchen.

At last, the bread was ready!
The Red Hen called out, "Who
will eat the bread?"

The Cat said, "I will."
The Rat said, "I will."
The Pig said, "I will!"

The Little Red Hen said, "No, you won't. I will."
And she and her chicks ate every tasty crumb.

The Eagle

He clasps the crag with crooked hands;
Close to the sun in lonely lands,
Ring'd with the azure world, he stands.

The wrinkled sea beneath him crawls;
He watches from his mountain walls,
And like a thunderbolt he falls.

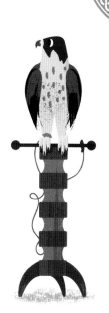

The Echoing Green

The sun does arise,
And make happy the skies.
The merry bells ring
To welcome the Spring.

The sky-lark and thrush,
The birds of the bush,
Sing louder around,
To the bells' cheerful sound.
While our sports shall be seen
On the Echoing Green.

Old John, with white hair
Does laugh away care,
Sitting under the oak,
Among the old folk,
They laugh at our play,
And soon they all say.

"Such, such were the joys.
When we all girls & boys,
In our youth-time were seen,
On the Echoing Green."

Till the little ones weary
No more can be merry
The sun does descend,
And our sports have an end:

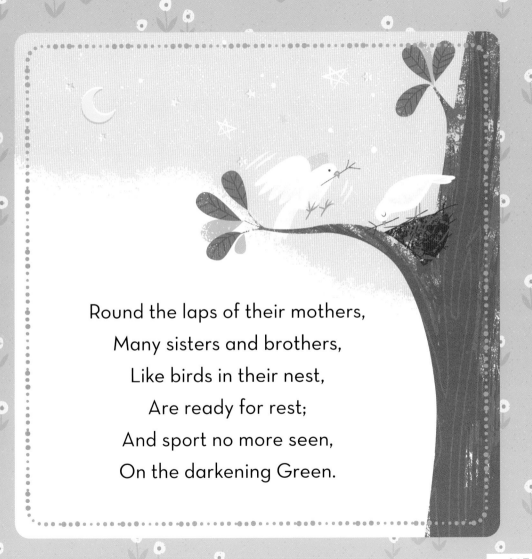

Round the laps of their mothers,
Many sisters and brothers,
Like birds in their nest,
Are ready for rest;
And sport no more seen,
On the darkening Green.

little grasshopper books™

The Three Billy Goats Gruff

Once upon a time there were three billy goats, and their last name was Gruff. They lived in a valley high in the mountains.

There was Little Billy Gruff. He was the smallest.
There was Middle Billy Gruff. He was a little bigger.
And there was Big Bill Gruff. He was the biggest.

The three billy goats liked to eat fresh green grass. But they had eaten all the grass in the field. There was nothing left to eat.

A mountain river rushed past the field.
On the other side was a meadow where
sweet green grass and flowers grew.

The billy goats could not swim across the river. But the meadow looked so green! Over there they could eat and eat and eat.

There was an old stone bridge that crossed the river. It was wide enough for a single billy goat.

But there was a grumpy, hairy, hungry troll living under that bridge. He did not like anyone. He especially did not like anyone crossing his bridge.

The three billy goats walked to the river. "Maybe we could cross over that old stone bridge," they said.

"I will walk over," Little Billy Gruff said. "The bridge is wide enough for me. And I am getting very hungry."

"Trip, trap, trip, trap," went the little goat's hooves. The grumpy, hairy, hungry troll heard the sound. "Who is sneaking over my bridge?" he cried.

"Only me," Little Billy Gruff said. "I am going over to the meadow."

"No, you are not. I will eat you first!" said the troll.

"I am too small to eat. Wait for the next goat—he is much bigger," said Little Billy Gruff.

"Oh, very well," said the troll.

Next came Middle Billy Gruff. "Trip, trap, tromp, tromp," went his hooves. "Who is sneaking over my bridge?" cried the grumpy, hairy, hungry troll.

"Only me," Middle Billy Gruff said. "I am going over to the meadow."

"I will eat you first!" said the troll.

"I am not much to eat. Wait for the next goat—he is much bigger," said Middle Billy Gruff.

"Oh, very well," said the troll.

Next came Big Bill Gruff. "Clomp, bomp, clomp, bomp," went his big hooves. "Who is sneaking over my bridge?" cried the grumpy, hairy, hungry troll.

"It is I, Big Bill Gruff. And I am not sneaking!"
"Now I will eat you!" said the troll.
"Oh no, you will not!" Big Bill cried.

The grumpy, hairy, hungry troll opened his
mouth and roared. He ran at Big Bill Gruff. But Big
Bill Gruff did not run away. He lowered his head and
charged. He butted the troll right off the bridge.

The troll fell into the river and was carried away. He was never seen again.

Big Bill Gruff joined the other billy goats. They went to the meadow full of sweet green grass and they ate and ate and ate. They are probably still there.

There Was a Crooked Man

There was a crooked man, and he walked a crooked mile,
He found a crooked sixpence against a crooked stile,
He bought a crooked cat which caught a crooked mouse,
And they all lived together in a little crooked house.

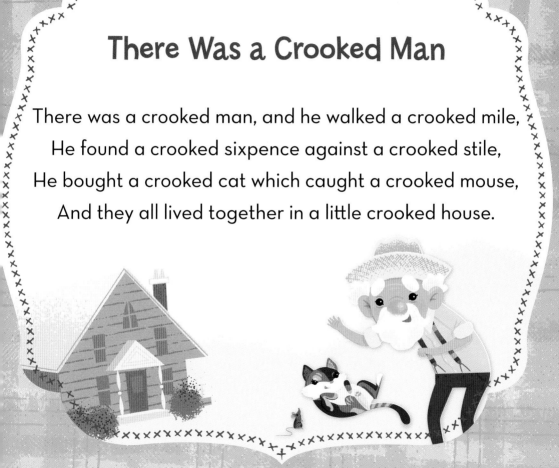

The Moon

The moon has a face like the clock in the hall,
She shines on thieves on the garden wall,
On streets and fields and harbour quays,
And birdies asleep in the forks of the trees.
The squalling cat and the squeaking mouse,
The howling dog by the door of the house,

The bat that lies in bed at noon,
All love to be out by the light of the moon.
But all of the things that belong to the day
Cuddle to sleep to be out of her way,
And flowers and children close their eyes
Till up in the morning the sun shall arise.

Twinkle, Twinkle Little Star

Twinkle, twinkle little star,
How I wonder what you are.

Up above the world so high,
Like a diamond in the sky.

Twinkle, twinkle little star,
How I wonder what you are.

Ladybird, Ladybird

Ladybird, ladybird,
Fly away home,
Your house is on fire
And your children all gone;

All except one
And that's little Ann,
And she has crept under
The warming pan.

Peter Rabbit

Once upon a time there were four little rabbits named Flopsy, Mopsy, Cotton-tail, and Peter. One morning their mother said, "I am going to the baker's. You may go down the lane, but don't go into Mr. McGregor's garden."

Flopsy, Mopsy, and Cotton-tail were good. They went to pick blackberries. But Peter was naughty. He ran straight to Mr. McGregor's garden!

First he ate some lettuce and some beans. Then he ate some radishes. Then he went to look for some parsley. Next to the parsley was a cabbage patch.

Peter saw Mr. McGregor kneeling in the cabbage patch, planting cabbages. And Mr. McGregor saw him!

Mr. McGregor jumped up and ran after Peter. He called out, "Stop, thief!"

Peter was very scared. He ran around the garden. He had forgotten the way back to the gate.

Peter lost one shoe in the cabbage patch, and then the other in the potatoes. So he ran on four legs and went faster. He ran so fast that he did not see a berry net in front of him. Peter got caught in the net.

He tried to get free, but his jacket buttons were stuck. Mr. McGregor saw Peter in the net. He almost caught him, but Peter wiggled out of his jacket and ran.

Peter rushed into the toolshed and jumped into a watering can. It was wet!

Mr. McGregor came into the toolshed. He began to turn the flowerpots and look for Peter under them.

Right then, Peter sneezed. "Achoo!"

Mr. McGregor was after him again. Peter jumped out of a window.

Peter was out of breath and very scared. He did not know where to go. He found a door in a wall. But it was locked. There was no room to squeeze under it.

Peter saw a mouse, carrying peas and beans to her family. Peter asked her the way to the gate. She did not know. Peter cried and cried.

Peter came to a pond. A white cat was staring at some goldfish. She sat very still, but now and then the tip of her tail twitched. Peter thought it best to go away without speaking to her.

He went back towards the toolshed. But suddenly, he heard the noise of a hoe—scritch, scratch, scratch, scritch.

Peter hopped under some berry bushes to hide. When nothing happened, he climbed on a wheelbarrow to try to see the garden gate.

The first thing he saw was Mr. McGregor hoeing onions.
His back was turned towards Peter. Beyond him was the
gate!

Peter ran as fast as he could to the gate. Mr. McGregor saw him, but Peter did not care. He slipped under the gate and was safe at last. Peter never stopped running until he got home.

Mr. McGregor hung up the little jacket and the shoes for a scarecrow to frighten the blackbirds.

Peter did not feel well. His mother put him to bed with
a cup of chamomile tea. Flopsy, Mopsy, and Cotton-tail
had bread and milk and berries for supper.

Star Light, Star Bright

Star light, star bright,
First star I see tonight,
I wish I may, I wish I might,
Have this wish I wish tonight.

Gathering Leaves

Spades take up leaves
No better than spoons,
And bags full of leaves
Are light as balloons.

I make a great noise
Of rustling all day
Like rabbit and deer
Running away.

But the mountains I raise
Elude my embrace,
Flowing over my arms
And into my face.

I may load and unload
Again and again
Till I fill the whole shed,
And what have I then?

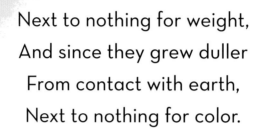

Next to nothing for weight,
And since they grew duller
From contact with earth,
Next to nothing for color.

Next to nothing for use,
But a crop is a crop,
And who's to say where
The harvest shall stop?

Time to Rise

A birdie with a yellow bill
Hopped upon my window sill,
Cocked his shining eye and said:
"Ain't you 'shamed, you sleepy-head!"